First published in the United States in 2018 by
Eerdmans Books for Young Readers,
an imprint of Wm. B. Eerdmans Publishing Co.
Grand Rapids, Michigan
www.eerdmans.com/youngreaders

Manufactured in the United States of America

29  28  27  26  25  24  23  22  21          3  4  5  6  7  8  9  10  11  12

**Library of Congress Cataloging-in-Publication Data**

Names: Lewis, Gill, author. | Weaver, Jo (Children's author), illustrator.
Title: A story like the wind / by Gill Lewis ; illustrated by Jo Weaver.
Description: Grand Rapids, MI : Eerdmans Books for Young Readers, 2018. |
  Summary: As a group of refugees huddles together in a rubber dinghy in the
  middle of the sea at night, one of them uses his violin to tell a story of
  how the instrument was invented and of a white stallion that ran like the
  wind, weaving their stories together and giving them hope for freedom in
  the future.
Identifiers: LCCN 2018002547 | ISBN 9780802855145
Subjects: | CYAC: Refugees—Fiction. | Storytelling—Fiction. |
  Violin—Fiction.
Classification: LCC PZ7.L58537 Su 2018 | DDC [Fic]—dc23 LC record available at
https://lccn.loc.gov/2018002547

# A Story Like the Wind

WRITTEN BY
## GILL LEWIS

ILLUSTRATED BY
## JO WEAVER

EERDMANS BOOKS FOR YOUNG READERS

GRAND RAPIDS, MICHIGAN

A boy is slowly spinning through space.

For fourteen summers and thirteen winters he has lived on earth.

    He is tall and thin, his coltish legs too long for a body that has yet to catch up.

    He has dark hair, dark eyes, and a mouth that once held a smile.

    It is a boyish face, a thousand years old.

    He wears jeans and a T-shirt and a red silk scarf.

    He cradles a long, slim case against his chest.

    It is all he has.

    It is all he has left.

*I am nothing,* he thinks.
*Just a handful of stardust.*
*But if I am nothing, how*
*can it hurt this much?*
He can still see his
mother in bright morning
sunlight. His feet can still
run the maze of dusty streets.
He can still trace his name
etched in the top of his school desk.

But all that is gone.

They are only memories,
moments of light locked
into his synapses, and
pockets of time spilling
away to the stars.

They belong to another lifetime.
Not to the now.

Maybe this is what it is like to die.
To be ripped away.
To leave behind everything you have ever loved,
unable to return.

He glances at his fellow travelers, their faces ghosted by the moon.

They sit in a circle, their knees cramped up to their chins, clutching the remains of their lives in small bags.

A man and wife sit together, their arms wrapped around their two young children.

Beside them, an old man carrying a small white dog.

And two boys, with the dark shadow of manhood on their faces.

They are all strangers to him, strangers who by their leaving have joined him too. They are bound together, floating across time and space, to the promise of a safe harbor of a different world.

The outboard motor gave up some time ago.
It spluttered its death rattle.

A last cough.
A last breath.
Then silence.

Leaving them without maps,
without oars,

spinning,

spinning,

spinning,

slowly beneath the stars.

In a small boat,

with a small hope, in a rising wind,

on a rising sea.

The wind and waves begin to dance, kicking up cold salt-spray. The boy runs his fingers along the goosebumps that rise on his bare arms.

He is real.

He is here.

Here is now.

*I am alive*, he thinks. He tilts his head back and speaks to the stars. "My name is Rami, and I am still alive."

Another voice speaks into the night.

"You look cold, Rami."

The young mother has spoken. She offers her knitted shawl. "Here, wrap this around you."

Rami pulls his red scarf tighter around his neck and shakes his head. "Thank you, but I am warm enough."

The woman's eyes rest on Rami. "My name is Nor," she says, "and this is my husband, Mustafa."

Mustafa lifts his head from his hands and manages a weak smile. He has been sick since leaving land.

Nor pushes stray wisps of hair beneath her headscarf. She rests her hand on each child in turn. "This is my son,

Bashar. He is six. And my daughter, Amani, who is four."

Bashar's eyes are wide and round. His eyebrows jump as each wave thumps against the boat. Amani is curled beside him, escaped in sleep.

Both children are wrapped in thick coats and blankets. They are the only ones with life jackets in this boat, which is not a boat. It is a toy, a plaything for beaches and swimming pools. Two layers of plastic and air are all that lie between its passengers and the bottom of the sea. A belt buckle or loose hairpin could tear it apart. A ride on this small dinghy is as expensive as a cabin on a cruise ship. One-way tickets, a thousand dollars each.

"My name is Mohammed," says the old man. He strokes the ears of the shivering dog tucked inside his coat. "And this is Bini. It's been a long time since she was a puppy, and even longer since I was a boy, but we still have each other."

"My name is Youssef," says the older of the two boys. "And this is my brother, Hassan. We have been traveling for many days now." He looks across at Rami. "We are also still alive."

The words tumble from the passengers' lips, eager to etch their names into each other's minds.

Remember me.

Remember my name.

Mohammed pulls a folded flatbread from his bag. It is wrapped in paper, like a gift. Rami cannot help but stare. Saliva forms, thick and sticky in his mouth.

"Here," says Mohammed, tearing strips of bread and passing them around to each passenger in the boat. "Eat. It is a long time until dawn."

Rami shakes his head. "Thank you, but I am not hungry." He watches the others chew the bread, while his own stomach cries out for food.

The waves rise and fall, and the boat tilts and slides. Mustafa groans and sinks deeper in the boat. His feet belong to the land, not to the sea.

Youssef holds up a plastic bottle. "Have some lemonade. Our mother made it for us before we left. It is made from the lemons that grew on the tree in our backyard." He passes it to Mustafa. "Take a sip and pass it around. Mama said lemons are good for seasickness."

When the bottle reaches Rami, he does not drink, but passes it on to Mohammed. "Thank you, but I am not thirsty."

Youssef looks at him. "What is it, Rami? Why don't you share our food and drink? Why do you refuse to wrap Nor's shawl around you when we can all see you are cold?"

Rami's hands grip the slim case against his chest. "I have nothing to give in return. This is all I have left."

Bashar's eyes open wide. "What's inside?"

Rami unclips the lid and opens the case. "This," he says.

A violin lies sleeping in a bed of dark velvet, with a bow resting alongside. It looks out of place here.

Too fragile.
Too intricate.
Too beautiful.

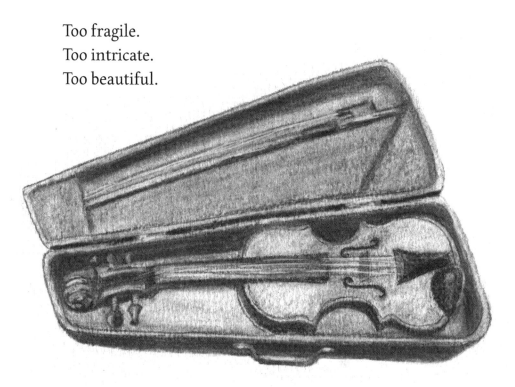

Suspended silence from some other world.

Rami lifts it with two hands as carefully as if it were a newborn child. "I had to leave quickly," he says. "I took the only thing I could not leave behind."

Bashar wriggles over to Rami for a closer look. He reaches out to touch the curled scroll and the pegs holding the taut strings in place, and traces his finger along the slender neck and the smooth wooden curves of the violin's body.

Youssef looks into the empty case and frowns. "This is all you have? You have nothing to eat?"

"No," says Rami. "Just this."

Hassan shakes his head. "What use is it to you now? You could have sold it for food, or water, or even a life jacket."

Rami shakes his head. "No. You see, this is everything to me. It carries my soul."

Mohammed leans forward. "Please show us, Rami. Show us what this means to you."

Rami lifts the violin to his chin and pulls the bow from the case. "You see, it remembers many stories." He draws the bow along the strings, and a deep melody fills the night. "It remembers the time before the war, when the morning sun rose over my father's wheat fields, lifting the mist and turning them to gold. It remembers warm nights and the music we played in our village after the harvest, and the smell of coffee and roasted almonds."

Bashar reaches up into the air as if he is trying to catch the music, but the notes slip and slide away on the wind.

Rami smiles and lets the bow wobble across the strings. "It remembers my audition to join the symphony orchestra, and how nervous I felt. It remembers the joy of its own voice joining that orchestra as we grew to learn other stories."

Nor puts a hand on Rami's arm. "Maybe you could play for us and tell us one of your stories. I would like to hear one. The night is long, and it will help to keep the darkness away."

Rami rests the violin on his knees and pulls at a loose hair on the bow. "I would not know which one to tell."

The sea writhes beneath them, folding and bending their boat. The plastic seams pucker and creak.

Nor's hand tightens on his arm. "Tell us a story to see us through this night," she whispers, her eyes bright with tears. "Please tell us a story that will carry us into the dawn."

"I do have a story, but it is a dangerous one," says Rami, running his fingers along the grain in the wood. He frowns. "The conductor of the orchestra told it to me on the day the soldiers came. The soldiers forbade us to play more music. Perhaps they knew its power. Perhaps they knew what it could do. The conductor gave me money and told me to run. I had no time to return to my family." Rami lifts the end of the red silk scarf. "He also gave me this to remember. He asked that I wear it, whether I play in alleyways or town squares, or in the greatest music halls of the world. He said everyone must hear this story."

"Then please tell it to us," says Mohammed. Bini peers out from beneath his coat, her dark eyes watching Rami.

"Yes," says Hassan. He and Youssef slide forward in the boat, their arms hugging their knees, like much younger boys. "We would like to hear it too."

Mustafa wraps his arms around his wife and children.

There is a lull in the storm, and even the sea seems to pause to listen.

Rami sits up on the edge of the boat, the silk scarf streaming out behind him. He lifts the bow to the strings. "This violin can play many songs," he says. "But it also carries an ancient tune. It remembers the First Story in the grain of wood of its body, in the tautness of its strings, and in the scroll of its neck. No religion or nation can claim the story for its own.

"It belongs to us all.
It is the song of freedom.
It is a story like the wind."

"How does it begin?" whispers Bashar.
Rami smiles. "I am about to tell you."

Together, they all turn their backs on the restless waves and listen.

In a small boat,
with a small hope,
in a rising wind,
on a rising sea.

"This story begins many, many years ago," says Rami, "on the high plains of the Mongolian desert, a place known as the land of a million horses.

"It begins with the galloping of hooves across the plains." Rami drums his fingers on the wooden body of the violin, and thundering hoofbeats fill the night.

He takes his bow and slides it across the strings. "It begins with the wind blowing down from the high Steppe mountains, bringing the first chill of winter and the first flakes of snow."

The music rises and falls with the swirling wind.

"It is the story of Suke, a young shepherd boy who was herding his sheep down from the mountains. It begins with something he found in the snow."

"What did he find?" whispers Bashar.

Mustafa pulls Bashar into his lap. "Shh! Bashar. Let Rami tell the story."

Suke was the youngest of three brothers, all of them eager to find shelter ahead of the storm. Even their horses picked up the pace, their tails tucked and their heads bent against the wind. Light was fading, and the valley below was deep in shadow.

"Suke," called the oldest. "I can see some of our sheep on the high slopes. Your horse is the youngest and fastest. Go and herd them up while we take the rest of the flock home."

Suke muttered beneath his breath and turned his horse around, while his brothers made their way down toward the light of the yurts. He grumbled to himself. They would be sipping warm mare's milk long before him.

He looked up to the high peaks shrouded in cloud. Snow had already filled the ravines and gullies. Autumn was over, and the elders predicted hard months ahead. Suke's horse picked its way along a narrow track clinging to the steep side of the mountain. Loose stones and shale skittered over the edge and disappeared into the swirling mists. But Suke knew to put his trust in his horse. He turned his face skyward while soft snowflakes fell, melting on his cheeks like winter's first kiss.

Suke urged his horse up a steep ravine toward the last stragglers of sheep, his horse high-stepping through the deep drifts of snow.

The ravine became narrower and steeper, patterned with blue shadows, bending and folding over snow-covered boulders. Suke's horse became tense and skittish beneath him, head high and nostrils flaring. Suke squinted into the light, snow-blind to the dark spaces between the rocks. Were there wolves? They hadn't been seen on these mountains for years. He stroked his horse's neck. "What is it?" he whispered, trying to comfort himself as much as his horse. If there were wolves, they would be trapped here with nowhere to run.

His horse snorted and pawed the ground. Then Suke saw the contours of another horse on the ground, the snow lying deep over its body. Suke jumped down and wiped the snow away from the horse's face. It was a mare, but she was quite dead. Ice crystals sparkled on her long dark lashes. It was too late to help her. Suke tried to lead his own horse past, but his horse would not move. It bent down and pushed its muzzle into the drift of snow, blowing warm air through its nostrils. Something moved beneath the snow. Suke knelt and dug down with his hands to find a small foal curled against its mother. The foal was cold, but Suke could feel its soft eyelids blink as he ran his hands across its face. He scooped the snow away until he could see its small white head. Foals this small rarely survived the winters, and this one surely would not survive without its mother. Suke looked around to see if there were other horses on the mountain, but except for the wind moaning through the gullies and whistling between the rocks, the mountainside was cold and silent.

Suke wiped the snow clear from the foal. Its coat was as white as the snow, and its eyes as dark as the night sky. Its wet mane and tail were both short and frizzled. It couldn't be more than a few weeks old. Suke felt its nose and slipped his fingers inside its mouth. Its tongue was cold and dry, and the foal too weak to suck. He tried to lift it to its feet, but it had no strength left within it to stand. It would not survive the night out here, and there was more snow on the way.

Suke gathered the small foal up in his arms and lifted it onto the saddle of his horse, covering it with his own coat. He led his horse down from the mountain, herding the stragglers of sheep ahead of him.

"What took you so long?" His father was waiting for him at the head of the valley. "I was coming to find you."

"I found an orphaned foal on the mountain."

Suke's father lifted the edges of the coat and examined the small foal. "A little colt," he said. "It's one of the wild horses."

"He needs food and warmth," said Suke.

His father shook his head. "It is too weak. It will not survive the night."

"I will try," said Suke. "He is not dead yet."

And so Suke took the foal into the warmth of the yurt, where he laid him down in front of the fire.

Suke's grandfather knelt down to inspect the foal. "He belongs to the wild herds. Even if you keep this foal alive, you will never tame him."

Suke's brother prodded the foal with his toe. "It will be dead by morning."

Suke ran his fingers across the foal's soft muzzle, and bent to whisper in his ear. The foal's small ear twitched as he spoke, and Suke knew the foal was listening. "You won't die. I promise. I won't let you die."

"And what will you name your foal?" asked Suke's mother, handing him a bowl of warm stew.

Suke stared long and hard into the foal's dark eyes. "It is not for me to give him a name. He belongs to the wild. He belongs only to himself."

Grandfather nodded. "And so it is. But if you are to save him, you must first give him some milk. My own mare had a late foal and still has milk. Take some from her, and I will help you feed this foal."

Suke stayed awake the whole night, feeding warm milk to the foal, letting it suck from a milk-soaked skein of wool. As dawn pooled through the skylight, Suke finally fell asleep beneath a pile of soft blankets, curled around the white foal, cradling its head against his chest.

As he slept, he dreamed the foal became the wind, prancing around him, and however fast he ran he could not catch it. Even when he raced the wind to the very ends of the earth, the foal somehow slipped beyond his reach.

Bright sunlight woke Suke from his sleep. He shielded his eyes from the slant of light silhouetting Grandfather in the open doorway. He reached for the foal, but his arms were empty. Had the foal died in the night? Had the foal slipped from his hold? Was it all a dream?

Suke sat up and rubbed his eyes. "The foal . . . ?"

Grandfather held out his hand and chuckled. "Come and see . . ."

Suke followed him outside to see the small white foal standing beside Grandfather's old mare. The foal's head was hidden beneath the mare's flank, but his tail waggled to show he was drinking her warm milk.

Grandfather put his arm around Suke. "I was sure this young foal would be dead by morning," he said. "And I have seen many foals over my years. This one has great strength within. If he lives, he will grow to be an extraordinary horse."

Bashar tugs Rami's arm, stopping the flow of music. "Did the foal live?" he asks, wide-eyed.

Rami smiles. "It takes a lot of time to look after a sick foal," he says. "But most of all, it takes love."

Nor wraps her arms around her son. "It was the same with you, Bashar, when you were born. You arrived too early, and the doctors said you would not survive. But your father and I fed you and carried you and looked after you, and you lived. They said it was our love that kept you alive."

Rami smiles. "This violin knows many stories about love. It knows many kinds of love. It can tell the story of first love too." He draws the bow across the strings, weaving two melodies. The notes tease each other, pull apart, and flow together.

Mustafa reaches for Nor's hand and holds it in his.

"It remembers the first time lovers meet and the first time they dance. It remembers their hopes and dreams," says Rami.

Nor squeezes her husband's hand. "Maybe it knows our story," she says. "Do you remember the first time my father let you take me out?"

Mustafa smiles. "We went to the theater, but I don't remember the movie."

Rami plucks the strings with his fingers. "It remembers the first kiss."

Nor and Mustafa smile, but Bashar pulls a face. "But what about the foal? Did he die?"

Rami shakes his head.

"The foal did not die. He lived."

In its first year, the foal followed Suke wherever he went, trotting alongside him as he tended the horses and sheep. As Suke grew from a boy into a man, the foal grew into a stallion, with a coat as white as the whitest snow and eyes as dark as the darkest night. He would let only Suke ride him. Without saddle and bridle, they galloped across the plains. Together, they would race the wind and chase the setting sun to the ends of the earth.

Word of the white stallion spread across the land, and many came to admire him. They offered money and gold to Suke, but Suke would shake his head and reply each time, "He is not mine to sell. He belongs only to himself."

In the white stallion's fifth summer, the clans prepared for the great race across the plains.

"Will you enter?" asked Suke's brother as they rode together to the gathering.

Suke nodded. "Only if the white stallion is willing to carry me."

They arrived in the evening as the sun was setting behind the mountains. Music and the smell of roasting nutmeg and cinnamon swirled into the air. Suke had to grip tightly to the white stallion's mane as they trotted through the markets, past stalls and horse sellers, past carpet sellers, yurt makers, and saddlers. Torches burned late into the night as people bought and sold and bartered, each person demanding a good price.

Rami lets his bow trip
back and forth, the notes
sliding and jostling with
each other, faster and
faster, bringing the light
and color of the marketplace.
The notes haggle and chatter
while Rami's fingers dance along
the strings.

Mohammed claps his hands in time with the beat of
Rami's music, keeping pace with the busy market song,
with Bini yapping excitedly in his arms. He taps his foot and
breaks into a smile.

Remembering.

"This is my story," he says. "It reminds me of the markets
at home where I was a carpet seller. People came from far
and wide to buy my carpets. It was a game in the market, a
dance between the seller and the buyer, haggling for the best
price. Those were the days." The corners of his eyes crease
into lines of laughter. "I once tried to sell a flying carpet to a
beautiful woman."

Rami stops playing. "A flying carpet? You tried to sell a
flying carpet?"

Bashar's mouth drops wide open. "A real flying carpet?"

"Oh yes," smiles Mohammed. "Many years ago, when I was a young man, a woman with eyes as deep as the ocean and a smile as warm as the sun came to my stall. She wanted to buy one of my carpets. She was the most beautiful woman I had ever seen, and so of course I fell deeply in love with her at first sight. I said, 'I have only one of these magical carpets, but I am willing to give it to you on one condition.'"

Nor tips her head to one side. "And what was the condition?"

Mohammed wags his finger at Nor. "I said to her, 'This flying carpet will take you anywhere you wish to go. Anywhere. It will let you live your dreams. But if you buy it, you must let me come with you.'"

Nor smiles as if she already knows the woman's answer. "And did this woman buy your carpet?"

Mohammed shakes his head sadly. "No, she didn't. I remember her words as if they were yesterday. She said, 'I have no desire to leave my home. And the only dream I have is to find someone to love me, and to give them my love in return.'"

Youssef shakes his head. "I'm sorry. That is very bad luck."

Mohammed's mouth breaks into a wide smile. "It wasn't bad luck for me. I became the luckiest man alive. She didn't buy my carpet, but she did become my wife."

Hassan laughs and nudges his brother. "Maybe we should try to sell flying carpets too!"

Mohammed strokes Bini's ears. "No woman on earth could be loved as much as I loved her."

Bashar looks around the people in the boat and tugs at Mohammed's sleeve. "Where is she now?"

Nor puts her arm around

her son. "Hush, Bashar. Enough questions."

A wave slams into the side of the boat, stinging them with cold spray.

Mohammed tucks his small white dog beneath his coat, sheltering her from the wind. "Bini is my wife's dog," he says. "Now we only have each other." He holds up a key that hangs by a piece of string around his neck and touches it to his lips. "This is the key to a door that no longer exists, the door to my house that is nothing but rubble. In my dreams my wife still lives there. When I unlock that door, I see her waiting for me." Mohammed slides the key beneath his shirt and closes his eyes tight shut. "She still holds me, in my dreams."

The wind whips his words away and carries them over the water, leaving empty spaces in the silence.

"Please," says Mohammed, opening his eyes, "continue the story, Rami. Tell us, did Suke ride his stallion in the race?"

Rami lifts the violin to his chin and begins to play.

The next day, the fastest horses of the land stood stamping and snorting, pulling at their bits in the dawn light, their breaths misting in the cool air. Steam rose from their glistening flanks. The riders wore their finest clothes, decorated with fox furs and eagle feathers, and the horses wore tack embroidered with colored thread. Only Suke was dressed in shepherd's clothes, sitting on the back of the white stallion who wore no bridle or saddle at all.

As the horses lined up for the race, the richest lord of the land arrived on his black stallion, wearing black furs and spurs of gold. He was flanked by armed guards, whose metal armor reflected the rays of morning sunlight like sharp blades into the crowd. People parted to let them through.

Suke's brother pulled Suke aside and whispered, "Let the Dark Lord win this race. He has an evil temper. If you cross him, he will increase our taxes and move us from our land."

The white stallion pawed the ground, impatient to be off.

Suke laughed and gripped the white stallion's mane. "Nothing will stop this horse. Look, he wants to race. Maybe it's time to see what he can do."

"Suke," called the brother, but it was too late.

The starting horn had blown, and the line of horses disappeared in a cloud of thundering hooves and dust.

The white stallion kept pace with the other horses, matching their strides with his easy gallop. The land rolled beneath them, across grassland, through rivers, up mountains, and down valleys. Always the Dark Lord and his black stallion were far out in front. As they descended the last mountain, Suke could see the bright flags and banners of the finish line far away on the plain. He could see the crowds awaiting the horses' and riders' return.

Suke let the white stallion pick his way down the last of the steep mountain trails. The Dark Lord was already galloping flat out across the plain, a dust trail far, far in the distance. Surely the Dark Lord would win, and Suke was glad, for he knew his family couldn't afford to pay more taxes. But the moment the white stallion's feet touched the soft grass, he tossed his head and raced after the black stallion. The white stallion was galloping faster than he had ever galloped before, his hooves thundering over the ground, his mane and tail streaming out behind. The earth spun beneath them, and it felt to Suke as if they were flying.

The black stallion heard the white stallion at his heels, put his ears back and pushed even faster, but the two horses were soon side by side. Head to head, shoulder to shoulder, they raced. The Dark Lord fixed Suke with his stare, urging his horse faster, but the white stallion kept pace with the other horse.

"Faster," shouted the Dark Lord, bringing his stick down on the black stallion's flank. He lashed it again and again, horse sweat and blood mixing together.

The white stallion flowed beside the Dark Lord like the wind.

"Faster," screamed the Dark Lord, digging his sharp golden spurs deep into the black stallion's sides.

But the black stallion had nothing left to give. His nostrils flared, and his lungs strained for air, but his big heart could give no more, and he fell, rolling and tumbling just short of the finish line, while the white stallion and Suke sailed past, the finishing flags streaming out behind them.

But there were no cheers or applause.

No horns or drumbeats to celebrate.

Just silence.

Breath-held silence.

And motes of golden dust suspended in the still, cold air.

The crowd watched as the Dark Lord picked himself up from the ground and brushed the dirt from his cloak. He walked slowly toward Suke and the white stallion, his face as dark as gathering storm clouds.

"Because of you, my finest horse is dead," he said.

The white stallion tossed his head and flattened his ears.

The Dark Lord narrowed his eyes and stared at Suke. "You will give me your horse in repayment for the death of mine."

"No," said Suke, daring to speak against the lord. "He won the race."

Suke could hear murmurs of agreement in the crowd behind him.

The Dark Lord spun around, and as he turned the crowd fell silent, and people turned their eyes to the ground. None dared look at him.

"If you do not give me your horse," roared the Dark Lord, "I will double everyone's taxes in my kingdom. If you do not give me your horse, I will order my guards to burn your home and move you from the valley into the mountains."

The Dark Lord's guards drew their swords and surrounded Suke and the white stallion.

The white stallion tossed his head and pawed the ground.

Suke slipped down from the horse's back. "I cannot give him to you," he said. "For he is not mine to give. He belongs to no one. He belongs only to himself."

"Guards," called the Dark Lord, "seize the stallion."

The white stallion reared and kicked out his hooves, but there were too many guards. They threw ropes around him and cast him to the ground.

"No!" shouted Suke. "You cannot ride him. It is for him to choose his rider." He tried to reach the white stallion, but the guards pushed him back.

The Dark Lord pulled Suke by the scruff of his cloak and pushed his face close to Suke's. "I am the finest horseman in the land. There is no horse I haven't broken. What is so different about this one?"

"He is like the wind," said Suke. "However hard you try, you cannot tame the wind. He is like the setting sun. However fast you travel, it always slips beyond your grasp."

The lord spat in Suke's face. "You dare to mock me?" He turned to face Suke's family. "Be gone from this valley before nightfall, or I will order my guards to fire burning arrows on your home and take every horse you own." He looked around at the people gathered. "And if anyone should help Suke, I will banish them too."

Suke fell to his knees and sobbed as he watched the white stallion being dragged back to the Dark Lord's citadel.

The crowds silently dissolved into the night as Suke and his family packed up their belongings. No one stopped to help them.

"You fool," shouted Suke's brother. "What have you done? Why did you not let the Dark Lord win as I told you to?"

Suke's father shook his head. "The mountain winters are too harsh. This is the end for us."

Grandfather held out his hand and pulled Suke to his feet. "No," he said. "The white stallion is the first to stand up against the Dark Lord." He rubbed his chin and stared into the distance, to the citadel silhouetted on the horizon. "I have a feeling this is only the beginning."

Inside the citadel, the Dark Lord tried to break the white stallion. He beat him and lashed him with a whip until the white stallion was streaked red with blood, but still the horse would not be tamed. The Dark Lord tried to bridle him and put a saddle upon him, but the stallion bit and kicked and would not let him near.

"I will break you," threatened the Dark Lord. He tied him in the sweltering heat and withheld food and water. The sun rose and fell, and the summer wore on, and the white stallion's coat became dull and gray, and his ribs and hip bones showed through his coat. His eyes lost their shine and sparkle. The stars inside them died.

The Dark Lord walked a circle around the white stallion, prodding him with the end of a stick. "Can you kick now?" he said, bringing the stick down on the horse's flank.

The stallion's legs buckled, and he struggled to stand.

"Can you bite?" roared the Dark Lord, forcing the metal bit of a bridle into the white stallion's mouth.

He called for his guards to saddle the white stallion. "Now come, let me show my people how I have tamed this horse."

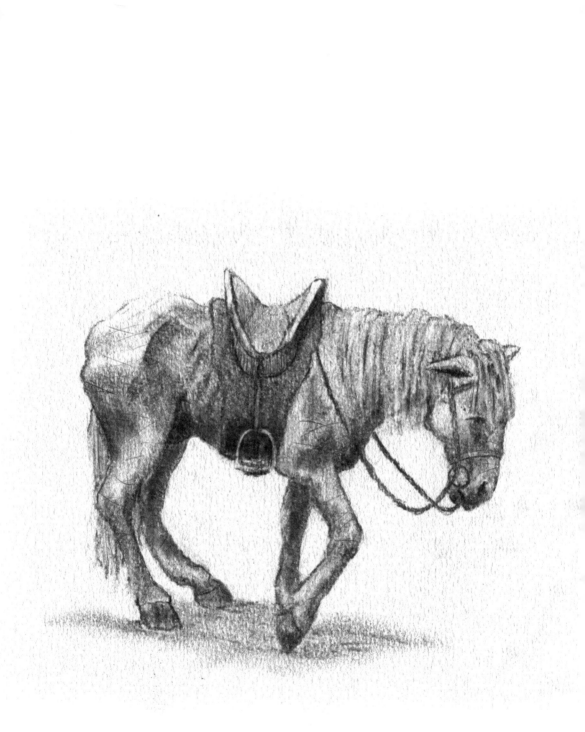

When the people saw the Dark Lord and his soldiers coming, they bowed their heads and stood silently watching him pass. Dark-eyed children peered out from behind their mothers, their faces sallow and gaunt. Their stomachs were hollow and starved by the Dark Lord's taxes. The white stallion walked with his head lowered, his mane and tail hanging in thick matted clumps. His brittle hooves scuffed the dry earth.

"You see," said the lord to his guards and the people, "there is nothing I cannot tame. I am the master of all."

The white stallion's legs trembled. He could feel the weight of the Dark Lord's body on his back and the sharp spurs against his sides. He closed his eyes and felt the first snowflakes of winter. A cold wind flowed down from the mountains and lifted the ragged ends of his mane, bringing a memory of the wide open plains. It brought the memory of the boy who had saved him, the boy who raced with him and chased the setting sun to the ends of the world.

The white stallion lifted his head to the cold wind from the mountains. He could hear it calling his name. He could feel it flow through him and give him strength in his legs and in his heart. He reared to answer its call, throwing the Dark Lord from his back.

"Catch him," the Dark Lord cried as he tumbled to the ground.

But the guards couldn't hold him. The white stallion kicked up his hooves and thundered toward the distant mountains.

"If I cannot have him, then no one can," roared the Dark Lord. "Fire your arrows," he ordered his guards. "Take him down."

And arrow after arrow rained down as the white stallion galloped into the darkness of night.

The clouds break and moonlight shines down on the passengers in the boat, reflecting in the tears on Youssef's face.

"You are telling the story of our home," says Youssef, wiping his cheeks.

Hassan nods. "Home was once a place where we used to play football in the dusty streets."

"Home was a lemon tree in the backyard," says Youssef, "and Mama making baklava in the kitchen to sell at the bakery. Our house was filled with the scent of honey and spices."

Hassan inhales the memories. "We used to do our homework at her table and wait for her to finish cooking, when she would let us run our fingers around the bowls and lick the syrup from the spoons."

Youssef nods. "It was the safest place in the world, that kitchen. Even from Ahmed, the school bully."

Hassan laughs a hollow laugh. "Remember the time Ahmed chased us back from school, wanting to take your new football? I had never seen him scared until Mama stormed out of the house. She was smaller than he was, but she marched him home and left him with words burning his ears."

Youssef stares at his hands. "It is not safe now. When the soldiers came, Ahmed joined them. He drove around the streets in a big car with a big gun. Not even Mama could tell him what to do."

"The soldiers asked Father to join them," says Hassan, "but he refused."

Youssef frowns. "One night the soldiers came for the men in our town. Father said we had to run. Mama packed us baklava and lemonade, and we headed into the mountains with other men and boys from the town."

Youssef puts his head in his hands. "But Ahmed found out about our escape and told the soldiers about our leaving. The soldiers followed us in trucks. Father and two other men told us to run ahead while they led the soldiers another way."

"We watched the soldiers follow them far away into another valley," says Hassan.

"There was gunfire," says Youssef, closing his eyes. "Lots of shooting. It sounded as if the mountains were being broken apart."

Hassan shakes his head. "But Father and his friends had no guns of their own. They ran into the darkness with bullets raining down on them."

"You see, Rami, your story is our story," says Youssef.

Nor nods. "This is the story we all share."

Bashar looks between Hassan and Youssef, and then at Rami. "But what about the white stallion? Did Suke ever see him again?"

"Shh!" says Mustafa. "Let Rami tell us in his own time."

Rami lifts the bow, and the notes spill out like tears into the wind, picking up the story.

High in the mountains, Suke woke to hear the clattering of hooves across the stony ground. He padded out into the night, and beneath the full moon, he saw the white stallion coming to meet him. But the great horse was weakened. His flanks heaved with the effort to breathe. He stumbled and sank down at Suke's feet.

Suke knelt beside him. He gently pulled off the bridle and saddle and cradled the stallion's head against his chest. "Stay with me," he whispered. "Stay, and I will look after you like I did before." But the stallion's breaths came short and shallow. The arrows had driven deep into his flesh. "Stay," begged Suke. He stroked the stallion's soft nose. "You are free to race the wind and chase the setting sun again." But Suke knew deep in his heart that the white stallion could not hold on to life. The stallion's eyes closed, and he died in Suke's open arms.

Suke fell asleep curled around the white stallion, crying hot salt tears into the night, while snowflakes spun down from the heavens, weaving a soft blanket of snow.

As Suke slept, the white stallion came to him in a dream. He appeared before him, his coat whiter than the whitest snow, and his eyes darker than the darkest night.

"Come," said the stallion.
"Ride with me one last time."
And so Suke climbed on the
stallion's back and rode with him
across the night, racing the wind to
the very ends of the earth.

As the first light of dawn crept into the sky, the stallion returned Suke to the mountain. "Remember me," he said. "Remember my name."

"But I don't know your name," cried Suke.

The stallion nuzzled him gently in the chest. "You do. You have it right here."

Suke's fingers gripped the stallion's mane. "I can't lose you."

"Then take one of my rib bones and some hairs from my tail to make a bow."

"To fire arrows?" asked Suke.

"No," said the stallion, shaking his head. "This bow will send forth something more powerful than any arrow." The stallion looked deep into Suke's eyes. "When you draw the bow across the hollow shell of my body, you will hear my song. You will share my story."

Suke woke and did as the stallion had told him. All day he sat and crafted an instrument from the bones and the hide in the image of the white stallion.

He stretched the hide across the stallion's bones, to become the body. When he drummed his fingers on the taut skin, the stallion's hoofbeats echoed across the mountain.

Suke cast tightened strands of horsehair from the neck to the tail of his new instrument, and when he rode the bow across these strings, the sound of the wild wind flowed around him.

Finally, Suke carved a piece of bone into the shape of the proud arching head of the white stallion. To always remember him. To never forget.

As night fell, Suke played the white stallion's song. The wind carried the music over the mountains and down into the valleys, where it swirled into villages and flowed in through doors and windows. People stopped to listen, and soon they were humming its tune and tapping their feet to its rhythm. The blacksmiths beat it out with their hammers on their anvils. Mothers hummed it to their unborn children, and men sang it while plowing their fields. It carried over the walls of the citadel and right into the Dark Lord's house.

"Stop," ordered the Dark Lord. "Stop this music." But he couldn't stop the music. The wind carried it and whispered it into his ears. It called to him from the fields. It came rushing down with the raging rivers from the mountains. "Go and find who is making this music," he ordered his guards.

His soldiers set out on their horses. They heard the song everywhere, yet they could never find the maker of the music. "It is the wind, master," they said on their return. "It comes with the wind."

"Then catch the wind," roared the Dark Lord.

"But sire," pleaded the soldiers. "No one can catch the wind."

"Then we will shut the wind out," raged the Dark Lord. He ordered that all the houses in the citadel should have their windows and doors sealed with tapestries, but still the wind carried through the fine weaves of the fabric. The servants secretly danced to it as they swept the floors. Caged birds sang it, remembering the sky. Even the soldiers heard the song. They hummed it in their sleep and began marching to its rhythm.

"Shut it out," roared the lord. He covered his ears, but still he could feel the music throbbing through the walls and floors of his house. He ran down to the dungeons, but he could still feel the music through the earth. "I need to go deeper," cried the Dark Lord. "Bring me a spade."

The Dark Lord dug into the dark soil, farther and farther, tunneling into the earth away from the music.

Deeper

and deeper

and deeper.

Where the Dark Lord ended up, nobody knew.

Some say the tunnel walls collapsed on him. Others say he is still down there, digging. But some say he is biding his time, waiting for the song to stop, ready to return.

The news of the Dark Lord's disappearance traveled far and wide. The celebrations spread from the citadel to the mountains. And when Suke's family returned to the valley, the people crowded around Suke to see the maker of the music.

"This is the white stallion's song," said Suke, drumming his fingers on the body of the instrument and drawing the

bow across the strings. And it was as if the white stallion was galloping alongside them, racing the wild wind. "You see," said Suke, "even in death he could still defeat the Dark Lord."

Soon people wanted to make their own instruments too. They made them out of wood and took hairs from their own horses' tails to make the strings and the bow, and they carved a horse's head for the top of the instrument. They called it the morin khuur, or the horsehead fiddle. They learned to play the song, to tell the story too.

And the horsehead fiddle learned new stories—about love and friendship and grief and loss. It sang at weddings and parties and grieved at funerals. It traveled on the silk routes and spice roads across the world. It traveled into different lands, where people made it their own. They changed its shape, making it smaller or bigger, and they added more strings. They crafted violins that could be carried under the arm and double basses taller than a man. They played them in alleyways and town squares and music halls.

But one thing remained the same. They always carved a scroll, like an arching horse's head, in memory of the First Story, of Suke and the white stallion.

The song of freedom.

A story like the wind.

Rami's music spills out across the waves to the eastern horizon, where a pale light is breaking with rays of a promised sun.

"Thank you, Rami," says Nor, her arms wrapped around Bashar and Amani. "I will sing it to my children so that they may sing it to theirs."

Mustafa nods. "When I find work as a teacher again, I will sing it to my students."

The two brothers cling to each other. "We will never forget," says Hassan. "Never," says Youssef. "We will sing this story in memory of our father, who gave his life so we could live."

Mohammed strokes Bini's ears. "My wife would have loved to hear it. So I will sing it for her. I will sing it to keep alive the memory of the home we had, so that no one will forget. We need to remember, so that when this war is over, families can return and rebuild their homes and their lives. I will sing it to remember the busy markets and the coffee houses. I will sing it to tell the stories of my friends and neighbors. I will sing it for my wife, because she showed me that when everything is taken away, it is love that still remains."

Rami nods. "We must all sing it for those we have lost or left behind. We must sing it to those who do not know they need it yet. We must keep the song alive."

And together, they sang the song of freedom while their hearts beat out its rhythm.

In a small boat,
with a small hope,
in a rising wind,
on a rising sea.

**Gill Lewis** is a veterinarian and acclaimed children's book author. Her previous books include *One White Dolphin* and *Wild Wings* (both Atheneum), both of which have won the Green Earth Book Award. She lives in England with her family and their collection of pets, including a rescued Shetland pony. Visit her website at www.gilllewis.com.

**Jo Weaver** is an illustrator living and working in London. She holds a master's degree in children's book illustration from Anglia Ruskin University, and her books have been translated into seven languages. Her previous books include *Little One* (Hodder), which was long-listed for the Kate Greenaway Medal in 2017. Visit her website at www.joweaver.co.uk.